For Mark, James, Joe and Jess J.H.
For my mum, a rather wonderful woman. xxx S.J.

First published in Great Britain in 2012 by
Piccadilly Press Ltd, 5 Castle Road, London NW1 8PR
www.piccadillypress.co.uk

Designed by Simon Davis
Printed and bound in China by WKT
Colour reproduction by Dot Gradations

ISBN: 978 1 84812 237 6 (h/b)
ISBN: 978 1 84812 236 9 (p/b)

1 3 5 7 9 10 8 6 4 2

Who Loves Baby?

By Julia Hubery

Illustrated by Sean Julian

Piccadilly Press • London

Baby's asleep in his beautiful pram (at last).
Mummy and me are snuggled up reading
(but not for long).

Oh-oh, here it comes:
Ding-Dong!

It's the Gooey Gang.
They love Baby.
They hustle and bustle and fill up the room.
They chatter and natter and tread on my toys.

And then they start to goo.
"Ickle fingers!"
"Tickle toes!"
"Angel face!"

Don't they know Baby is icky
and sicky and pongy and pooey?
I hide behind the sofa and shut my eyes,
ever so tight, because I'm not in the Gooey Gang.

But I can still hear them.
Baby starts to whuffle.
"He's waking up!" they goo.
"Little snuffler!" they coo.

Don't they know Baby
cries and wails and whinges?
I put my fingers in my ears,
because I'm not in the Gooey Gang.

Mummy picks Baby
out of his pram,
and cuddles him.

The Gooey Gang gushes in.
"Can I have a little hold?" they goo.
"And me?"
"And me?"

I go upstairs to talk to Teddy.
I tell Teddy everything, and Teddy always listens.
"I don't like the Gooey Gang," I say.
"And I don't like babies."
Teddy doesn't like babies either.
They chew his ears.
But I do like Baby's new pram.

"Do you want to ride in it?" I ask Teddy.
Teddy would like that very much.

We wait till the Gooey Gang goes away.
Then we creep into the living room,
Teddy and me, ever so quiet.
Baby's fast asleep in his pram – again!

Teddy gets in the pram.
He doesn't like Baby's silly orange bear,
so he pushes it out.
Teddy sits right next to Baby.
Suddenly, Baby's hand twitches.
Poor Teddy! His ears!
I try to rescue him,
but Baby's tiny fingers wrap
around mine.

They hold on tight like they'll never let go.
"I didn't know babies were so strong!" I say.

Teddy wonders who's got the softest hair
– him or Baby?
I wriggle my finger free and stroke their heads.
Teddy likes that.
I shut my eyes so I can
feel them better.

Teddy's head is
silky-smooth.
Baby's head is warm,
so warm,
and soft,
and sleepy.

When I open my eyes, Teddy's fallen asleep.
"Wake up, Teddy," I whisper.
But – oh no!
Baby wakes up instead.

His two little dark eyes open
wide as wide, and look at me.
And look, and look,
like they never
want to stop.
"Hello, Baby," I say.

Mummy tiptoes in, ever so quiet.
She strokes my head, and kisses my nose.
"Does Teddy love your baby?"
"Teddy didn't love him AT ALL, at first," I say,
"but I think they might be friends now."
He's not one of the Gooey Gang though.

Then we sit on the sofa,
cosy and snug,

and I hold my baby, while Mummy
reads ALL of us a story.